ACKNOWLEI

CW00858333

Dedicated to my wonderful edito ... ...u.y ~ ..~y~...
Thank you for sharing your love and mastery of the English language, for a lifetime of creative input and expression. To Charmelle for bringing these characters to life with your incredible graphic designs. To Muna for the suggestion of dragons and reading through early versions. To Zandile and Mrs Margaret E Thomas for adding your voice and grammarly expertise. To Paul Rogoff, thank you for teaching us all to think outside the boundaries and limitations we can often find ourselves in. To my siblings (especially in-laws) for putting up with my enthusiasm, your honesty, input and reading of numerous drafts have been truly invaluable. Also my incredible nieces, nephews, step daughters, Godchildren and students. You are a constant source of inspiration, demonstrating all that is creatively possible and good about the world. Your 'voice' is a source of endless opportunity and the passport to your destiny - use it wisely. To Jay Gregory, my amazing husband, thank you for introducing me to the more scientific elements of space, the planets and for all the awesomeness that you are. Finally to all who have supported by purchasing, reviewing and sharing this series.

Thank you.

Written by Clair F Gregory with Illustrations by Charmelle Givans

Princess Carolina

the Queen of the Countermelody

LIFE IS MUSIC

From an early age Princess Carolina, found the rhythm of activity in the palace of Scenicosia, a constant source of inspiration. The sound of music was such a draw that her tutors would ensure song was included in all her studies. Indeed they had discovered that committing facts to melody meant they would become securely imprinted in her memory too. Carolina would sing all day long and loved to bring voices together, the more parts singing different melodies the merrier. In fact she was known affectionately as the 'Queen of the Countermelody'.

Why countermelody you ask? Well you see the princess liked to create layers in her songs, a single melody alone would never do. Every tune was the building block for a 'countermelody' to be added. These would be sung together, complementing one another, just like the different parts played by the instruments in a band or orchestra.

One morning she rose from her sleep with a song in her mind, as she often did and called on those nearest to her to develop a few layers of countermelody. Before long she had Chef James out of the kitchen repeating the lines:

"Oh oh oh I'm singing in the kitchen, oh I'm singing in the peas."

"What a glorious feeling I am in the right key…"

Cherie her lady-in-waiting was given the line:
"Today is bright and bee - eee - ay - ooh - tiful."

The window cleaner, an android named Amelie, heard what was happening and slid down her ladder to join in. Using a couple of large spoons from the palace dining tables, Amelie played a percussive rhythm. Just as the princess thought this was starting to sound interesting her mother Queen Alexandria walked into the room.

THE HARMONIOUS GIANT

Carolina: "Good morning Mother. I am working on a new song. Would you like to hear it?"

Queen Alexandria: "I'd love to Dear, but first there is a pressing matter of great importance that I must share with you. Do you remember that trip we made to the planet of Orbis many years ago?"

Carolina: "Yes, and we met that amazing dragon called Xavier who sang and whistled so very tunefully. I remember he used his tail and wings so skillfully to play percussion. Such a friendly dragon!" Disappearing for a moment into that wonderful memory, Carolina said wistfully; "If only I had a tail…"

Queen Alexandria with a smile, replied: "Yes that's right. Well it's that dragon who needs our help."

The Queen went on to explain that Xavier had a cousin named Olu who had found himself in a bit of a pickle. The dragons would often sing together wowing audiences with their incredible voices. Queen Alexandria explained that knights had often come in search of an imagined 'terribly scary dragon'. However they would always leave impressed

by the dragons' musical prowess, finding they were actually very friendly and not terrible or scary at all.

Sadly, not everyone knew that the dragons were friendly, harmless and oh so incredibly talented. Some inhabitants of the galaxy thought the dragons were scary, because of their size and fearsome appearance. It didn't help that occasionally they would 'accidentally' breathe a little fire when suffering with hiccups. So Olu had been captured and locked away in a large empty castle. The secure fortress was purpose built and fixed into the side of a mountain on the planet of Adrift (meaning lost). Olu's captors could not see that he was kind and brave. It was so unfair, he had been judged purely because he looked different.

Xavier was beside himself with worry about his cousin, which gave him a terrible case of the hiccups. This meant he kept accidentally breathing fire, making him look even scarier. He was so upset he could no longer bring himself to sing and between hiccups even whistling was too much effort. He didn't want to give the people of Adrift any reason to be afraid, which is why he needed Princess Carolina's help.

A SONG TO SAVE A GENTLE SOUL

Princess Carolina thought "If only we can demonstrate to the people of Adrift that these dragons are kind, perhaps they will let Olu go free." She then remembered a song that Xavier had taught them whilst guiding them on a tour of Orbis.

Princess Carolina called together the strongest voices on the planet of Scenicosia and taught them the song that Xavier had taught her all those years ago. It sounded wonderful! Once they were confident, Princess Carolina decided it was time to add some 'countermelodies'. She sent the singers to planets across the galaxy where choirs were invited to add their own short repeated melodic patterns to the song. Once every planet's choir had prepared, Princess Carolina put all the countermelodies together and they sounded incredible, creating harmonies and rhythms that were 'out of this world'. It was time to request an audience with Han Hu, the leader of Adrift.

Han Ku was flattered to receive a visit from the beautiful princess of Scenicosia. Keen to make a good impression and knowing her love of music, he arranged a concert in honour of the princess and invited her to sing her favourite song in their 'Super Stadium' with state of the art acoustics.

THE BIG PERFORMANCE

When the day of the performance arrived the concert line up included gifted musicians from Adrift who provided some impressive acts, including stunning arrangements of popular songs. Everyone was excited! The moment came for Princess Carolina to sing and at her request the glass ceiling of the Super Stadium was opened.

All was quiet and Princess Carolina, standing alone in the centre of the stage, began to sing Xavier's song. Initially intrigued, Han Ku was convinced he'd heard this somewhere before… "But where?" he asked. As the princess continued to sing, suddenly many singers appeared in a circle around her. It was her choir from Scenicosia, joining her in the first melody of the song. Gradually the singers turned outwards one at a time, each gesturing up through the open ceiling towards a nearby planet, introducing more voices, adding a second, third and fourth melody. New melodies could be heard until the entire galaxy was filled with song, each beginning slightly after the other due to the vast distance the voices were travelling.

Voices echoed across the galaxy with melodies dancing around each other like butterflies on a summer day. This unexpected miracle of sound represented a galaxy of contrasting planets, each complimenting and enriching the other. Han Ku was amazed, the atmosphere was electric, such an exciting moment in the history of Adrift. Everyone was enthralled as the beautiful singing was heard across the entire galaxy and into the wider universe.

A CHANGE OF TUNE

When Han Ku awoke early the next morning, echoes of the singing could still be heard, as people continued busily with their daily lives. He declared this was such a wonderful collection of melodies. He called on the princess again because he wanted to reward the writer of the magnificent tune that had started it all.

The princess explained it was Xavier, the friendliest, most musical dragon in all of the galaxy, who had written the initial tune.

"But he's so big and scary!" Han Ku exclaimed. "One fiery sneeze and we shall surely die!".

"Not at all," exclaimed the princess. Carolina went on to describe the incredible time she and her parents had spent with the dragon when he had introduced her to his planet.

This surprised Han Ku as he had only ever heard stories about dragons in which they were terrifying. "I have to ask you this." Han Ku said. "How did you stop him from eating you?"

Princess Carolina was amused. "Xavier would never eat us;

he's strictly vegetarian. The only time you would need to be worried would be if you were a mushroom!" she said laughingly. "He really loves mushrooms, but I'm sure even a mushroom that squealed loudly enough would be allowed to go free."

Han Ku began to realise he had made a terrible mistake but he was still a little afraid of the dragons. Princess Carolina insisted he come with her to the darker side of the planet of Adrift to visit Xavier's cousin, Olu, in the castle. On arrival Han Ku asked the guards how the prisoner was doing.

"Well he seems happy enough." Said the guards, who were quite relaxed. "He's not touched any of the 'dragon food' we have given him. We thought he would eat live animals, but instead it would appear he has been making friends with them. He has been eating leaves off the surrounding trees, and those he can't reach through the windows have been collected for him, mostly by birds and mice who have been visiting him daily".

Han Ku was truly astonished, but still a little apprehensive, as they approached the imprisoned dragon. As they got closer Olu's face lit with a smile when he spotted the princess through his prison bars.

Olu: "Princess Carolina I am so pleased to see you. I see Xavier managed to get word to your palace. Thank you for coming to visit. It is so hard to change someone's opinion of you, even when it is not at all true. Do you think I'm scary?"

Carolina: "Not at all, Olu."

Olu went on to describe an incredible dream he had had. He dreamt the whole planet was singing one of Xavier's songs and could be heard across the whole universe. Choirs on every planet joined in and it was the most beautiful sound he'd ever heard. He said the dream had reassured him that everything was going to turn out alright.

After listening intently to Olu's account of what he thought was a fabulous dream, Princess Carolina explained what had happened the night before. Olu was astonished as Princess Carolina said that choirs from each planet had joined together adding their own countermelodies to Xavier's original song.

Carolina: "Olu now I need you to be brave. I have someone who would like to meet you."

Olu had an idea that this may be Han Ku and the princess rested her hand on his giant clawed finger to reassure him. Han Ku entered the room with tears in his eyes and exclaimed: "But you are not the fearsome dragon I expected you to be! All my life I was taught that dragons are scary creatures who eat people. This castle was built centuries ago, when one of our ancestors saw a dragon and wanted to protect the people from danger." He paused, remembering all the scary things he had been told about dragons. "I was so wrong, Olu. Can you forgive me?"

Olu began to cry too, unhappy about being locked away in this dark and dingy castle. Yet he was so glad to see that Han Ku realised his perception of him was completely wrong. So wrong in fact that he looked down and Han Ku was clinging to his webbed, clawed foot, sobbing.

"I forgive you, Han Ku." Said Olu in a gentle reassuring voice.

Han Ku hearing Olu's gentle voice and realising what was happening, rose quickly to his feet. Straightening his clothes, he called the guards, commanding the chains to be removed and Olu released from the castle. The guards rushed in, rather pleased because they had come to like Olu, and unlocked the heavy chains around his ankles.

Olu, Princess Carolina and Han Ku looked at one another. Princess Carolina, holding the elbow of Olu's wing on her right and linking Han Ku's arm on her left said "Shall we?" The three of them, walking together, left the grand entrance of the castle followed by a plethora of animals all happy that they had lived to see another day. Princess Carolina led them into the city where Olu gently lifted Han Ku onto his shoulder so he could address the large crowd who had gathered:

"These dragons are not the terrifying creatures we have been led to believe. We must welcome them and allow them to enrich our lives with their beautiful songs and kind hearts. He then turned to Princess Carolina and said, "You have been here for just a few days and already our planet is full of light and new beginnings. With permission of the King and Queen of Scenicosia we, the people of Adrift, ask if you would come and take the role of Queen here and teach us more about the wider galaxy."

GREAT CELEBRATION

At the coronation both Xavier and Olu escorted the princess to her new throne and were greeted with great celebration. They also sang beautifully, accompanied by choirs from across the galaxy.

Queen Carolina's first declaration was to rename the planet from Adrift to Accordia, as the dragons they once feared were now friends and they were of one accord. The people's previous proclamation or mission statement had been one of fear and read;

"Adrift we are, Adrift we'll stay,
and keep the fearsome dragons at bay."

With a hiccup, and a playful puff of smoke from his left nostril. Xavier joined in with the huge cheer which erupted as the new mission statement was read aloud by all the people of the newly named planet of Accordia:

"We may all sing to our own unique tune,
our stories may be different
but when our voices rise in song
we are of one accord."

22

The queen had seen a wonderful change in Han Ku, who now loved exploring the universe with his new friends Olu and Xavier. Queen Carolina and Han Ku became very close friends. They fell in love and married, much to the joy of the people of Accordia. Side by side they reigned, and would soon introduce a few more princes and princesses to the galaxy.

ACTIVITIES

Create an image of Xavier or Olu?
Hint: A small human, house or tree will help show the dragons' size.

Create your own counter melody?
Hint: Create a short tune (add some lyrics if you like), write another, get a friend to sing (or play) one, while you sing (or play) the other?

Have a go at writing the next chapter?
Hint: Maybe start by explaining how life changed for Han Ku after he realised that Olu and Xavier were not the scary dragons he'd thought them to be?

NOTES

NOTES

NOTES

ABOUT THE AUTHOR

Clair Gregory BA Hons (Open), Dip Art, Dip Music, PGCPSE Inclusion in Education (Open University). Clair has worked as a peripatetic music teacher with regular placements in over 25 Schools in the Midlands for over ten years, alongside private coaching and tuition in a range of settings. Her love of writing expands into song lyrics, the odd bit of poetry and stories exploring a wide range of the factors that impact and distinguish our place in the world.

"I am a creative being, my objective is to maximize my own creativity whilst bringing out the best imaginative productivity in others."

ABOUT THE ILLUSTRATOR

Charmelle Givans is a gifted Midlands based Graphic
Designer, see more of her work online at:
Charmellegivans.format.com
or follow her on Instagram at:
@CharmelleGivans

Princess Carolina the Queen of the Countermelody

By Clair F Gregory

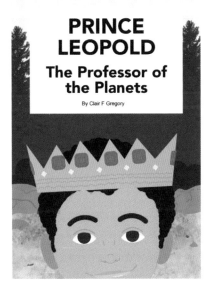

PRINCE LEOPOLD
The Professor of the Planets

By Clair F Gregory

Ruby THE Princess Choreographer

By Clair F Gregory

THE Princess AND her Books

By Clair F Gregory

ADVENTURES FROM SCENICOSIA

We hope you have enjoyed this fourth book from the series Adventures from Scenicosia, which follows the adventures of twelve siblings from a far away planet. Designed to encourage every reader to tap into their own full creative potential.

Look out for more books from this series...

The Princess and Her Books: Star Wars meets funky creative, mechanical engineer, princess. She may not find her handsome prince, but she does bring lasting change and peace to a feuding, war torn Galaxy.

The Princess Choreographer: When Princess Ruby was sent to govern the beautiful planet of Abundancea she found all was not well. The princess quickly discovered that her love of dance and skills as a keen choreographer could be utilised to bring about lasting change for a more harmonious planet.

Prince Leopold Professor of the Planets: Through the lens of his telescope Prince Leopold loved to gaze at the stars, discovering dinosaurs and the generation of a new planet, he builds on centuries of learning, exploration and discovery.

Princess Carolina, Queen of the Countermelody: The beautiful singing dragons of Orbis were a species truly misunderstood! They were nothing like the terrifying dragons of myths and legends. Proving many times to be peaceful and welcoming creatures, there was one crowd that needed a little help convincing.

Workout Wawina, Princess of Scenicosia, Queen of Opulencia: Using her kitchen garden irrigation system and the footsteps of her workout buddies. Wawina leads the people of Ravenoucia to a sustainable future. Her love of nutrition and her incredible drive to push beyond her personal best, in all things, leads her to nourish and energise all who care to join in.

Jehoshaphat Prince of Scenicosia, Knight of the realm: His artistic approach to life meant Jehoshaphat was rarely seen without a paint brush in hand or out exploring with his trusty steed Hubert. He worked closely with his twin sister Princess Wawina in the battle against hunger in Ravenoucia, developing his meticulous artistic skills to shape the landscape of many planets, enabling all to have access to clean water and spreading the source of the finest freshly grown produce into the wider galaxy.

Jaykob, Prince of the seriously small: BACTERIUM YUCKY-AND-STICKY-OSUM was just one of Prince Jaykob's discoveries. As he explored, through the magnifying lense of his microscope, he would become part of the hidden world of the extremely small. He loved to observe this secret world and soon found it played an important role in the lives of all.

Printed in Great Britain
by Amazon